FITH U

There is a Fire in the House

It Takes a Town

A. Tony Taylor

Printed in the United States of America, 2017

ISBN: 978-0-977-4231-6-3

www.fithuonline.com

Liberated Expression Publishing

www.liberatedexpression.com

Photography credit: Portia D.

FITH U

There is a Fire in the House

she begins.

The program was approaching its first ever Career Day.

(Silence)

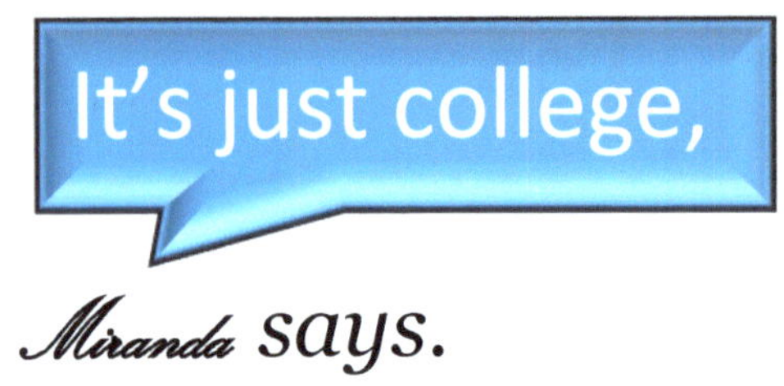

Miranda says.

Carl explains.

Miranda details.

(The two hear a knock at the door)

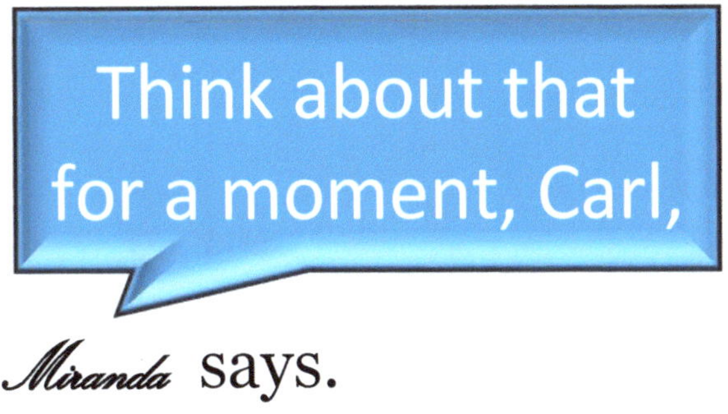

Miranda says.

Miranda exited the office.

There's an aspiring writer here. He wants to have a conversation with you. He's read your book— Beautiful Ashes,

Perris concludes.

Miranda re-entered the office.

Miranda inquires.

Carl asks.

Miranda clarifies.

Carl replies.

she says.

Carl urges.

He was enkindled by the thought of meeting his peers.

"A table for two"

These thoughts are ours.

Soon, we will meet.

We grow closer with every stroke

of a pen.

I will train once and sometimes

twice per day.

There isn't any room for error.

At Best, Tony

He joyously smirked. The letter was complete.

Willie says.

Nana asks.

Willie responds.

she says.

he ends.

the *presenter* states.

(Willie turns toward the television)

Willie considers.

He made one final adjustment to the tie he'd wear that evening. Once ready, Willie exited the apartment.

"We'll be back with more from FIX News—FITH Town's excellent source for all the updates you need to have," the *presenter* concludes.

 **<Conversations> (6)** +

the *server* says.

Ronnie announces.

Chan urges.

Taylor interrupts.

Willie says.

Taylor points out.

Trav responds.

Ronnie ends.

The pair approached a group of kids.

Miranda sparks a
conversation.

a *voice* emerges.

Miranda reveals.

...

she expresses.

the *voice* replies.

Welcome to FITH Shop,

Tony says to a customer.

Tony, what do you think about everyone leaving FITH Town?

Barry asks his coworker.

Tony replies.

Barry continues.

Tony concludes.

Tony exited the shop.

Ronnie says.

he insists.

Ron, you know you can't cook,

Taylor mentions.

In my spare time, I cook.
I'm not judging you…
don't judge me,

Ronnie states.

Sure, Ronnie, you can cook.
It might be Willie's big break,

Trav jokes.

Chan reveals.

(The mood settles)

Taylor asks.

They only wanted the best for one another. Eventually,
Willie and his former colleagues said their farewells.

The kids gathered together to discuss the rules of a
popular game in the community–*FITH's Missed.*

Lynn says.

he commands.

The wall was located near the entrance of the premises.

Lynn finishes.

Carl walked toward the wall.

a *voice* commands.

Willie calmly explains.

the *voice* pushes.

Willie pleads.

The voice ceased.

Willie quickly turned around.

He saw nothing.

he wonders.

Who would be held responsible?

a *voice* calls.

The egregious moment was just a dream. The inceptive despair escaped. A dense coolness took its place–air.

Willie asks.

Though Tony could see the uneasiness in Willie's demeanor, he didn't speak of it. Perhaps he knew why.

Tony jokes.

Suddenly, Carl was surprised by fire trucks leaving FITH Fire Station. He imagined himself going with the group. Finally, he rushed to tell Miranda of his encounter.

The weight on my shoulders will only make me stronger,

Willie declares.

Pain… I'm grateful for the pain. I've felt similar pain before,

he presses.

Tony, are you worn out yet?

Willie questions.

Tony says.

he challenges.

Willie finishes.

Drenched in sweat, the two turned to say their farewells.

Raff tells Carl.

Carl asks Raff.

Raff glanced at the program supervisors.

Carl rushed through the crowd of kids.

a familiar *voice* says.

Carl saw Lynn standing with Miranda.

Miranda says.

(The pair walks toward the facility)

Miranda states.

she asks.

(Silence)

Luke, I'm glad you're here in support of your colleague,

Chief says.

Chief, he is like a brother to me. We have always been there for one another,

Luke voices.

Chief asks.

How could he choose such a terrible time to tell a story?

Chief persists.

the *doctor* announces.

(The group stands at attention)

the *doctor* states.

Chief concludes.

That's not how the story goes. Your uncle was the one who was hurt that day. The crew showed up in support of Willie. I saw your mom there,

Tony explains.

Dad, I bet you're glad Uncle Willie—

Tony says.

the *daughter* asks.

Miranda clarifies.

the *son* asks.

I had it all figured out. I would train for years to become a better version of myself. I thought that I could impress her. After leaving the hospital, my car broke down. My roommate offered to give me a lift. That's when I saw her. She was walking with her hand in another man's back pocket,

Tony explains.

Dad, you took too long,

the *son* interrupts.

Son, you ought to be grateful,

Tony says.

Tell them what happened to your car,

Miranda insists.

After my car was towed to the nearest repair shop in town, I received a call from a guy by the name of Cody. He said,

"I have your problem, Tony."

It's out of gas.